Family By Love: A Story of Open Adoption by Kaycee Parker // Illustration by Emily Kay Rice.
Published by KP Communications. Copyright © 2017 by Kaycee Parker. All rights reserved.
No part of this book may be used or reproduced in any manner whatsoever without written
permission, except in the case of brief quotations embodied in critical articles and reviews.

For more information, visit FamilyByLove.com.

ISBN: 978-0-692-81422-2

A NOTE FOR PARENTS

Adoption today looks very different than it did 30, 20, or even 10 years ago.

The movement toward openness in adoption has had a dramatic impact on the lives of many families – both birth and adoptive families. Openness in adoption refers to various forms of communication between birth parents and adoptive parents. For instance, families might exchange letters and pictures with each other. They may even decide to meet one another face-to-face. Some families choose to share identifying information with one another while others choose to remain on a first-name-only basis. No matter the specific details of the relationship, there is an understanding and desire for ongoing communication and contact over the years.

As an Adoption Specialist, I have found many adoptive families initially approach the topic of open adoption with fear and caution. They often feel secrecy is necessary to protect their child as well as their own heart. However, as they learn more about the proven benefits of openness, not only for the birth family but even more for the adoptee, their hearts are often softened toward the idea. They begin to see the healing power that pictures and letters often provide for the birth family. They are able to witness the peace their child feels knowing where he or she came from and whom they resemble. I have seen firsthand the beautiful relationship that can be formed when both parties approach each other with open communication and trust.

If you are considering an open adoption, my hope is that you might be willing to take a step and dare to walk into the unknown of a new relationship with your child's birth family. Just like every relationship, it will be unique and not without mountains and valleys. But I believe you will find it to be unlike anything you've previously experienced.

Many blessings to you on your journey.

LAURA HAYS, BSW, MA
SOCIAL WORKER | CHRISTIAN FAMILY SERVICES, INC.

**As parents we must teach our children
love and compassion.**

There's no better way to do that than to share
with them the love and compassion of the Lord.

FAMILY BY LOVE
A STORY OF OPEN ADOPTION

BY KAYCEE PARKER // ILLUSTRATION BY EMILY KAY RICE

Hi! I'm Sophia.

I like to read books and swing at the park. I love to play with my fox named Scout. And I *really* like to play dress up!

This is Mama and Daddy. They tell me to
pick up my toys. And they tell me to eat my
vegetables. But we have lots of fun together.
I love them a lot!

One day, Daddy and Mama asked me
if I wanted to be a big sister.

Me? A big sister? That would be amazing!

Would the baby be a boy?

I could help him build a tower with my blocks. Or we could play outside in the sandbox together. A little brother would be super fun to swing with at the park!

Or would the baby be a girl?

I could paint her toenails pink. Or we could help
Mama bake our favorite cookies together. A little
sister would be super fun for playing dress up!

But Mama told me there wasn't a baby in her tummy.

I was confused.
"Then how can I be a big sister?" I asked.

Mama and Daddy sat down with me. "You know how you came from my tummy, Sophia? Well, your baby brother or sister will grow in another mama's tummy," she explained. "She will always be this baby's mother – his or her birth mother - and she will always be very important to our family."

She said, "Daddy and I have decided to adopt a baby who needs a loving family and a safe home - and a fun big sister just like you."

"In fact, Sophia," Daddy said, "God tells us we should love everyone, and we should take care of children who need our help. That's what we will get to do by adopting a baby."

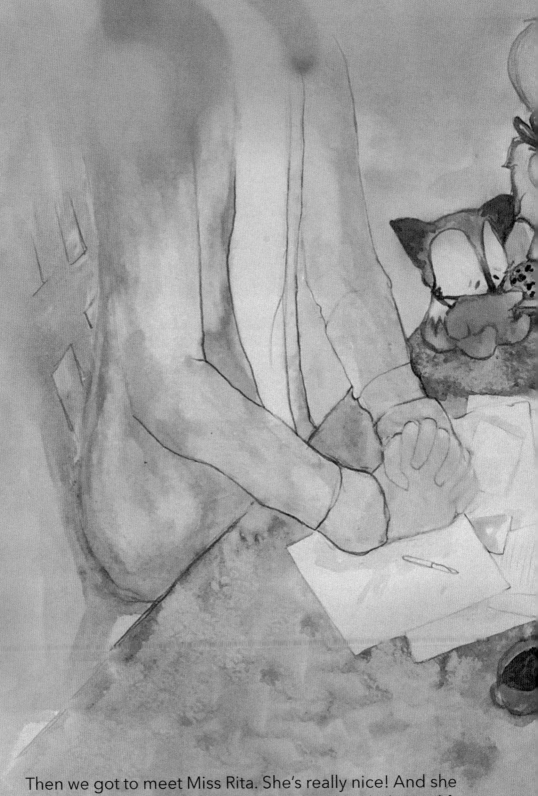

Then we got to meet Miss Rita. She's really nice! And she said she could help us find the baby God had planned for our family. She started coming to our house to visit us.

Miss Rita asked lots of questions to get to know our family.
And I got to eat a cookie every time she came over.
(Mmmm... chocolate chip cookies are my favorite!)

Miss Rita asked us to make a book all about our family. I love books, so I couldn't wait to help!

I got to pick out some pictures for our book.
My favorite was the one of us at the zoo.
That was a super fun day!

I even asked Scout which photos he liked best. We've had so much fun together.

When we finished making our book I said, "Miss Rita will really like our book, won't she?" But Mama said it wasn't for her.

"This book will be shared with the birth families who are ready to choose a family to adopt their baby and become their baby's forever family," she said. "Our book will help the birth families learn of all the fun things we like to do together. It helps them get to know us, just like Miss Rita did."

I liked that we got to share the pictures of our family. I asked Daddy, "How will we know when our baby is ready for us?"

Daddy smiled and said, "God builds families, Sophia. I know sometimes it's hard to be patient, but we just need to say our prayers and wait for the right time."

So we waited.

And we waited.

And we waited...

Thanksgiving came.
And then Christmas.
And even my birthday.

But we still didn't have our baby.
Was I ever going to be a big sister?

It was a warm spring day, and we all got in the car. Daddy and
Mama took me to the park to play and have a picnic lunch.
(Peanut butter and jelly for me!)

I rushed to the slide as soon as we got there. I even brought
Scout to slide with me.

At lunch Mama said she and Daddy had big news.
She said Miss Rita called, and we get to meet our baby
tomorrow! She said I'll be getting a baby brother.
His name is Louis!

I was SO excited! I was finally going to be a big sister! I
asked Mama if I could bring him a gift, and she said yes. I
couldn't wait to pick out something just perfect for him.

On Sunday morning after church, we all went to meet Louis.

I made sure to bring the present I picked out for him, too – a little fox just like Scout. I knew he would love it!

Mama and Daddy got to hold baby Louis right away. They even helped me hold him, too. I was so proud to be a big sister!

Then he got to come home to live with us. I got to sit right beside him on the way home.

Baby Louis doesn't look like me.

His skin.

His hair.

How can he be my brother
when we look so different?

Mama tucked me into bed that night after reading me a bedtime story - as always. *(I love to read my favorite poem book before bed!)*

She smiled at me and asked, "Well, sweetie, what do you think of being a big sister so far?"

Uh oh... I knew I had to tell her what I thought in the car.

I took a deep breath. "Mama, Louis doesn't look like me at all. How can he really be my brother?"

Mama smiled and held my hand. "You're right, Sophia. The two of you don't look much alike. But remember what Daddy told us earlier? God builds families. That means we don't have to look alike to be family," she said.

"God makes us all differently. Look at my hair, sweetie. It's brown and yours is blonde. But you're still my daughter and I love you. That's what *really* makes a family anyway – love." She kissed my forehead and said good night.

What Mama said that night was starting to make sense.
I knew Daddy and Mama loved Louis. I knew God loved
Louis. And I knew I loved him, too.

Mama even started calling me her big helper.
(I guess that means I'm learning to be a good big sister!)

I loved coming home from school each day to see my baby brother. We liked to play on the floor with our foxes. I loved reading my picture books to him.

I was really starting to like being a big sister. And I was really starting to like my new little brother.

"Sophia, let's finish up. It's time for bed, little miss," Daddy called.

I finished brushing my teeth. I ran into
my bedroom and jumped into bed.

Louis started crying in the other room.

Then Mama called, "Honey, could you help me please?"

"Uh oh," said Daddy. "Sounds like I should go help, Sophia. I love you very much. Get a good night's sleep, and I'll see you in the morning."

He kissed my forehead and turned off the lights.

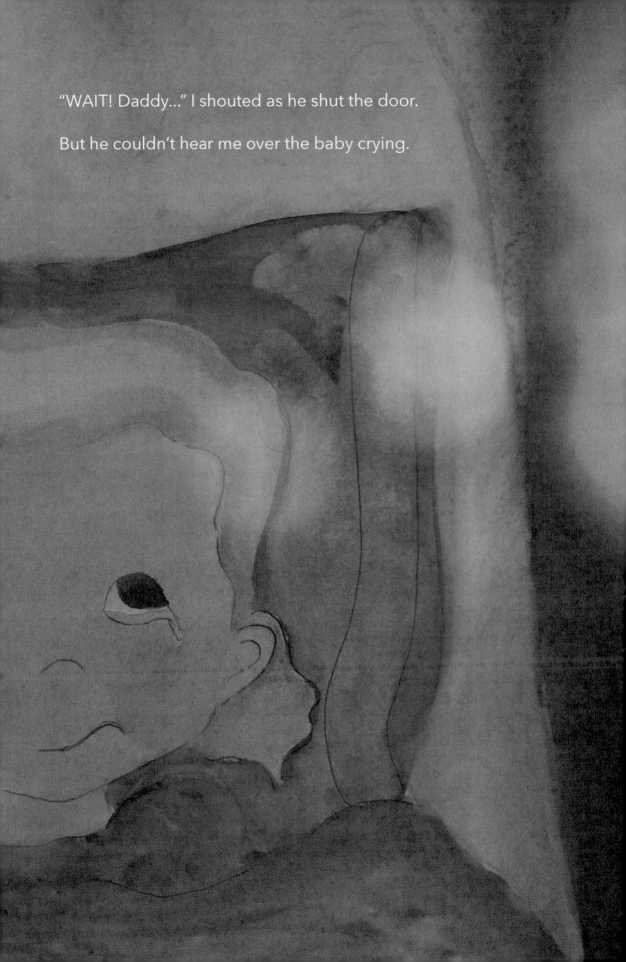

"WAIT! Daddy..." I shouted as he shut the door.

But he couldn't hear me over the baby crying.

Daddy forgot my story.

But we *always* read a bedtime story.

Maybe with Louis here now
Mama and Daddy don't have
enough time for me anymore.

I hugged Scout, curled up under
the covers, and closed my eyes.

The next morning I sat down at the table for breakfast before school. "Daddy, you forgot my bedtime story last night," I reminded him.

"Oh, you're right, Sophia. I'm sorry," he apologized. "We'll be sure to read one tonight, ok?"

"Maybe," I said, frowning. "Unless Mama needs help with Louis again."

Mama heard me. She came in to talk with Daddy and me.

"Sophia, just because I needed help with your brother last night doesn't mean we love you any less," she explained. "You know we love you, right?"

I looked up at her eyes and smiled back at her.
"I know you love me," I said.

"We all love you, Sophia," Daddy said, giving me a hug. "Lots of things are changing now. Our family has grown! But we'll get through it together – because we love each other. We're a family, right?"

"Right," I said. And I smiled. I knew they were right.

Louis had been with us for a while now. Mama said it was time to tell Miss Jada, Louis' birth mother, how he was doing. Mama wrote her a nice letter and sent her a new picture of him.

I got to draw Miss Jada a picture of Louis and me. I bet she will be glad to get our letters and pictures. Mama told me I could draw her another picture to send with our letter at Christmas time.

Mama said, "We will always tell Louis about his birth family and his adoption story. We want him to be proud of where he came from and never feel ashamed. And we know these pictures will help Miss Jada know that Louis is well taken care of and loved by so many people."

Louis is growing really fast now.

We like to color and go to the park together.
And he lays on his tummy to play blocks with me.

He likes to play in our sandbox, too. And sometimes
he tries to put sand in his mouth. *Yuck!*

But do you know what? I think Louis is ok after all.
I'm really happy he's my brother!

Last week we had our family pictures taken.
Here we are - don't we look great together?

Maybe we can send this picture to Miss Jada.
I bet she would love it!

I really like seeing our new pictures.
It reminds me that love makes us family.

Made in the USA
Coppell, TX
01 August 2020

32080393R00026